For Virginia for choosing love
For Juliane for being there at the onset
For Thea for her fierce dedication to justice
And, of course, for all of us

When your heart is heavy

And
your
step
unsure

When the
winds
are wild

TRADIT
Hypothetical exam
Example compares
thereafter; "Catch-u
deferred account
IRA. Distributions
epth and brea
spectrum —th
is expertise
k needs. And
extraordinary
age, protect an
more integrated so
customized recommendati
we've been entrusted to m
years.
erienced advisors customize

And
the
path
unclear

Don't fear the night,

so dark and vast

Or the hazy future

Or the stormy past.

Know that I am here,

as steady as stone

WMAN AND ERBE MFG. CO.

MAIN FACTORIES AND EXECUTIVE OFFICES

ROCHESTER

nearest branch or agency or to our

1. name of
   on our Form 99 gumm
   surname first, followed
   Example: No. Z. DAV

2. On the tab of this folder
   put the same number that
   which this folder is
   L. This n thea is a

ould be filed in folder
g filed toward the
should be filed
correspond
h or Agent

Firm Name or Subject

ence

Date of

to run credit, less
collection, 4 %
27.
Paid De Veani + Hal
eight draft nine,
themselves for
half of invoice of 1
net, by check on
2

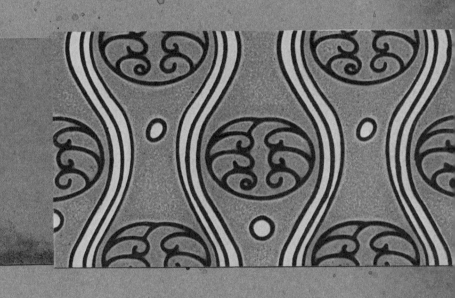

together

Than we are

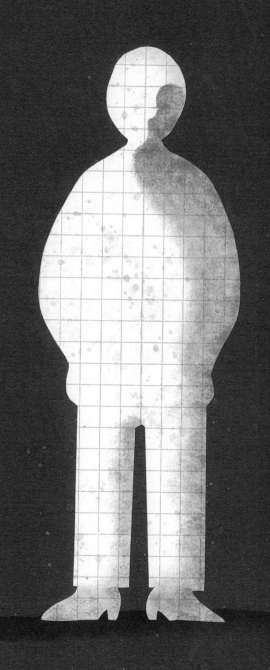

alone.

Hope and light will always prevail

For love wins.

Love wins.